Who Wins the Race?

written by Pam Holden
illustrated by Michael Cashmore-Hingley

Joe was going in a big race.
"I can go fast," said Joe.

"I can win this race!"

Joe went very fast.
He ran away from all
his friends.

Then he looked back to see
who was coming.
No one ran as fast as Joe.

He ran fast up the hill.
Then he looked back to see
who was coming.

No one ran as fast as Joe.

Joe ran fast into the woods.
Then he looked back to see
who was coming.

Oh, no! He fell down.
Crash! Ow!

All his friends ran
into the woods.

"Get up, Joe!" they said
as they ran.

They all ran down the hill.

But Tom stopped to help Joe.

Joe got up and
he ran with Tom.

They ran and ran to
get to their friends.

Joe and Tom ran fast,
and they won the race!